BARNEY IS BIG

by

NICKI WEISS

PUFFIN BOOKS

PUFFIN BOOKS
Published by the Penguin Group
Viking Penguin, a division of Penguin Books USA Inc.,
40 West 23rd Street, New York, New York 10010, U.S.A.
Penguin Books Ltd, 27 Wrights Lane, London W8 5TZ, England
Penguin Books Australia Ltd, Ringwood, Victoria, Australia
Penguin Books Canada Ltd, 2801 John Street, Markham, Ontario, Canada L3R 1B4
Penguin Books (N.Z.) Ltd, 182–190 Wairau Road, Auckland 10, New Zealand

Penguin Books Ltd, Registered Offices: Harmondsworth, Middlesex, England

First published in the United States of America by Greenwillow Books,
a division of William Morrow & Company, Inc. 1988
Published by arrangement with William Morrow & Company, Inc.
Published in Picture Puffins 1989
1 3 5 7 9 10 8 6 4 2
Copyright © Monica J. Weiss, 1988
All rights reserved

LIBRARY OF CONGRESS CATALOGING-IN-PUBLICATION DATA
Weiss, Nicki.   Barney is big / Nicki Weiss.   p.   cm.
Summary: Before going off to his first day at nursery school,
Barney and his mother recall what being a baby was like and discuss
what a big boy he is now.
ISBN 0-14-054059-8
[1. Growth—Fiction. 2. Babies—Fiction.] I. Title.
[PZ7.W448145Bar 1989]   [E]—dc20   89-32423

Printed in Hong Kong by South China Printing Co.
Set in ITC Quorum

FOR

GERI

STAN

TEDDY

JIMMY

RICKY

One morning Barney watched Mama
watering the flowers.
"I'm a big boy," said Barney.
"Yes, you are," Mama said.

"Tomorrow I'm going to nursery school," said Barney.
"Your very first day," Mama said. "There will be so
    many new things for you."
"And for you, too," said Barney.

Mama put down the hose.
"Barney, dear," she said, "I'm not going
to nursery school. You are."
"You won't be there?" asked Barney.

"We can walk there together and I can stay for
a little while," Mama said. "But then I'll go."
"Why can't you stay?" Barney asked.
"You're not a baby anymore," said Mama.
"You don't need me for everything."

That evening Barney was in the bathtub.
"Only babies need their mommies to do things,"
he said.

"Oh, yes?" Mama asked.

"Yes," said Barney. "I'm a big boy. I can wash myself."

Barney put on his pajamas.

"I can get dressed all by myself," he said.

"I can use a knife to push my peas on my spoon."

He got into bed.

"I used to help you do all those things,"
Mama said. "It takes time to learn how
to do things on your own."

Mama tucked Barney into bed.

"Tomorrow's the big day," she said.

"Are you ready?"

Barney pulled the covers up to his chin.

"Hmmm?" Mama asked.

"Let's pretend I'm a baby," said Barney.

Mama sat on the bed.

"Ga ga! Goo goo!" Barney said.

"You used to talk like that," Mama said. "You also used to sleep in a crib, and I would give you a bottle before you went to sleep."

"Let's pretend this cup is my bottle," Barney said.

"Sometimes you would put your thumb
in your mouth," Mama said.
"Like this?" asked Barney, and he stuck
his thumb right in.

"Yes, like that," Mama said. "And I used to rock
   you in my arms and sing until you fell asleep."
"Like this?" Barney asked.
   He crawled onto Mama's lap.

"Yes, like this," Mama said.
She started to sing.

"Sometimes big boys need to be babies, too."
she said.

Mama woke Barney early the next morning.
Barney got out of bed and washed himself.
Mama watched as he put on his clothes.

Then they went down to the kitchen, where Mama
poured milk into Barney's bowl of cereal.
"I'm going to nursery school today," said Barney.
"That's right," Mama said. "We'll walk there together."

"You can stay for a little while," Barney said.
"But then you have to go."
"And I'll be waiting right outside the classroom door
   when school's over," said Mama.
   Barney finished his cereal.

They got ready to go.

Barney put his hand in Mama's,
and they started on their way.

J Fic
WE

Weiss, Nicki

Barney is big.